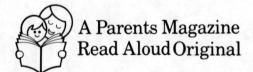

A Parents Magazine
Read Aloud Original

Those Terrible Toy-Breakers

David McPhail

Parents Magazine Press ● New York

For Shane

Library of Congress Cataloging in Publication Data

McPhail, David M.   Those terrible toy-breakers.
SUMMARY: Walter and Bernie set a trap for the
lion, tiger, and elephant who break Walter's
toys that are left outside overnight.
[1. Toys—Fiction.   2. Animals—Fiction]   I. Title
PZ7.M2427Th   [E]   80–10450
ISBN 0–8193–1019–0   ISBN 0–8193–1020–4 lib. bdg.

Walter lived in the jungle.
At least he thought it was the jungle.
It looked like it.
There were thick bushes
all around Walter's house
and big trees all around his yard.

Walter's friend Bernie told him once
that there were lions and tigers
and elephants out there.
So it MUST have been the jungle.

"But they only come out at night,"
Bernie said.
"They won't bother you in the daytime."

Walter didn't want to get eaten
by a lion or a tiger,
or stepped on by an elephant.
So he made sure that he had
all his toys picked up and
he was in the house before dark.

But one night Walter forgot
to put his tricycle away.

When he went out the next morning,
he found it all bent.

"What a terrible thing to do!"
said Walter to Bernie.

"A lion did it," Bernie said.
"You can tell by the claw marks
on the handlebars."

A few days later Walter kicked his
football so hard, he couldn't find it.

In the morning it was sitting
in the middle of the yard—
as flat as a pancake.

"Someone around here isn't being
very nice," Walter told Bernie.
"It's a mother tiger," Bernie said
after he looked at the ball.

"Those stripes on the ball
would fool a tiger and make her
think it was a tiger egg.
And of course she would sit on it
to try and hatch it."

Nothing else happened until Walter's
wagon got stuck in the garage doorway
while he was putting it away.

In the morning it wasn't stuck anymore,
but it was broken right in half.
Walter was angry.

"Who could do such a terrible thing?"
he asked Bernie.
"An elephant," said Bernie.
"Only an elephant's foot could break
a wagon in half like that!"

"All of my toys are being broken,"
Walter cried. "What can I do?"
"You've got to set a trap," Bernie said,
"and catch all those terrible toy-breakers!"

Walter didn't know how to set a trap.
He didn't even know what a trap was!
But Bernie showed him.

First they dug a big, deep hole
just below Walter's bedroom window.

Then they got some sticks and laid them
across the hole.

After that they covered the sticks
with leaves and dirt.

"There," said Bernie.
"Now all we need is some bait!"
And he looked at Walter's teddy bear.

"Not my teddy bear!" said Walter.
"But lions and tigers and elephants
LOVE teddy bears!" Bernie explained.
"Nothing else will do!"

"Then we won't do it!" Walter said firmly.

"Do you want those animals to keep breaking your toys?" Bernie asked.

"I'll HIDE all my toys!"
Walter said desperately.

"Then they'll get angry," Bernie said.
"And they'll come and eat you up!"

When Bernie put it that way,
Walter didn't seem to have much choice.
So he gave Bernie his teddy bear.
Bernie put it in the bushes above the hole.

"There!" he said, pleased with himself.
"To those animals it will look like
your bear fell out the window.
And when they come over to get it,
they'll fall into the hole!"

Then Bernie and Walter went up to
Walter's bedroom to wait.

Walter was almost asleep when
Bernie nudged him and whispered,
"Here they come!"

Sure enough,
a lion, a tiger, and an elephant
came out from behind the trees
and crept towards Walter's teddy bear.

The lion, who was leading the way,
was the first one to fall into the hole.

He reached out to grab a branch,
but he grabbed the tiger's tail instead,
and pulled HER into the hole, too!

"Get us out of here!"
they called to the elephant.
The elephant got down on his knees
and leaned into the pit.
"Grab on to my trunk," he said,
"and I'll pull you out!"

Both the lion and the tiger lunged for
the elephant's trunk and grabbed hold.
"One at a time!" shrieked the elephant.

But it was too late!
The weight of the lion and the tiger
together was too much for the elephant,
and he tumbled head first into the hole
on top of the two big cats.

What a commotion there was then!
"Get off me!" roared the lion.
"Me, too!" shouted the tiger.
"I can't!" said the elephant.
"I'm stuck!"

While all this was going on,
Bernie and Walter ran downstairs
and stood at the edge of the hole.
"Now we have you!" said Bernie with glee.

Walter lifted his teddy bear out of
the bushes and held on to it tightly.

"Are you the ones who broke my toys?"
Walter asked.
"Accidents," said the lion. "All accidents."

"We never meant to break them,"
insisted the tiger.
"We were just playing," added the elephant.
"Now help us get out of here!"

"Not until you promise to fix
Walter's toys," said Bernie.
"We promise," said
the lion, the tiger, and the elephant.

So Walter and Bernie took hold of
the elephant's trunk and pulled
as hard as they could.

Slowly the elephant climbed out of
the hole and plopped down on the grass.
"Whew! Thanks!" he said to Walter and Bernie.

Then he reached into the hole with his trunk.
"Now," he said to the lion and the tiger,
"try it one at a time."
And very soon they, too, were out of the hole
and on the grass beside Walter and Bernie.

Walter went back to his room
and returned with his tool box
and his broken toys.

True to their words,
the lion, the tiger, and the elephant
went right to work repairing the toys,
fixing them up as good as new.

"There," they said when they
were finished. "All fixed!"
"Thank you," said Walter.
"You did a wonderful job."

"You're welcome," they said.
"We're sorry we broke them."

To the elephant he gave his
cowboy hat, cowboy rope, and spurs.

And to his friend Bernie he gave
a pat on the back and a mug
of warm cocoa.

Walter felt so bad about trapping
the lion, the tiger, and the elephant
that he gave each of them a present.

To the lion he gave his
scooter.

To the tiger he gave his
striped beach ball.

ABOUT THE AUTHOR/ARTIST

DAVID MCPHAIL says of *Those Terrible Toy-Breakers:* "It is a simple, fun story. If there is a deeper meaning, it might lie in the nature of faith that one friend has in another. Walter wants to believe Bernie's explanations no matter how silly or far-fetched they seem. It's a story that had great appeal to the illustrator in me because of its many possibilities."

Mr. McPhail is the writer and illustrator of quite a few picture books for other publishing companies as well. To these occupations he has recently added that of farmer. He now lives on an 80-acre farm in New Hampshire that looks out on two mountain ranges and a pond full of frogs.